The Instagram Mom

My Baby Should Be...

Author

Connie M. Brandy

COPYRIGHT PAGE

NC Self Publishing Books

All rights reserved. No part of this publication may be reproduced, stored in a retrieval system, or transmitted, in any form or by any means, electronic, mechanical, photocopying, recording, or otherwise, without the prior written permission of the publisher, except for brief quotations embodied in critical reviews and certain other noncommercial uses permitted by copyright law.

© 2023 NC Self Publishing Books

Published by NC Self Publishing Books

Printed in USA

First Edition: 2023

Disclaimer: The information contained in this book is for general informational purposes only. The author and publisher make no representation or warranties of any kind, express or implied, about the completeness, accuracy, reliability, suitability, or availability with respect to the book or the information, products, services, or related graphics contained in the book for any purpose. Any reliance you place on such information is therefore strictly at your own risk.

Table of Contents

INTRODUCTION: 4

CHAPTER 1: THE WORLD OF FILTERS "BABY SARAH" 7

CHAPTER 2: THE QUEST FOR PERFECTION "LILY AND NOAH" 14

CHAPTER 3: THE ENVY TRAP "THE JEALOUS MOMMA" 20

CHAPTER 4: THE SOCIAL MEDIA COMPARISON GAME "ALEX" 26

CHAPTER 5: BEHIND THE SCREENS "THE REAL DEAL" 38

CHAPTER 6: REDISCOVERING AUTHENTICITY "JANE'S STORY" 44

CHAPTER 7: EMBRACING IMPERFECTIONS "THE TRIUMPHANT MOM" 54

CONCLUSION: 67

Introduction:

In the age of social media, where hashtags and filters reign supreme, a new breed of moms has emerged—the Instagram moms. These mothers embrace the digital world with open arms, documenting every precious moment of their child's life in picture-perfect squares and sharing them with the world. But behind what seemingly to be perfect scenes lies a deeper truth. The pressure to conform to an ideal image of motherhood. This book takes a deeper look into the worlds of Instagram moms who struggle with the unspoken expectations and explores what it truly means for their Children to be more than just a snapshot on a screen.

As we diver into the worlds of being an Instagram mom, we'll discover the unspoken expectations and pressures that come along with it. Behind the carefully curated photos and picture-perfect squares lies a constant battle to present an idealized image of motherhood. The pressure to conform to sociality standards and gain validation through likes and comments can be overwhelming.

Every milestone, from the first step to the first tooth, is captured and shared with the social media world. These moments, once intimate and personal, now become part of a public narrative. The joy of motherhood is often overshadowed by the need to portray a flawless life, where everything is picture-perfect and pristine.

But amidst the filters and hashtags, these moms find themselves questioning the true essence of motherhood.

They all wonder if their child's worth is reduced to a mere snapshot on a screen. Are they missing out on genuine connections and experiences by focusing solely on creating a curated digital persona? The quest for validation through social media can sometimes overshadow the joy of being fully present in the moment.

As these moms navigate the realm of Instagram, they realize the power of vulnerability and authenticity. Behind the scenes, they all grapple with sleepless nights, tantrums, and the inevitable messiness of parenting. They understand that real motherhood is a beautifully imperfect journey, filled with ups and downs that can't always be captured in a perfectly composed photo.

The Instagram moms embark on a journey of self-discovery, questioning their motivations and intentions. They find solace in connecting with other mothers who share similar struggles and challenges. Through open and honest conversations, these moms begin to redefine their perception of motherhood and find freedom in embracing imperfections.

Gradually, they all learn to strike a balance between documenting precious moments and cherishing them for themselves. They realize their child's worth extends far beyond the confines of social media and that true fulfillment lies in nurturing a genuine and loving relationship with their little one.

In this introspective journey, the Instagram moms rediscovers the joy of being present in the moment, celebrating the messy and unfiltered aspects of motherhood. They learn to prioritize their own well-being and that of their child over the expectations of others. With new found clarity, they now use social media as a tool for connection and support rather than a measure of their worth as mothers.

Chapter 1: The World of Filters "Baby Sarah"

As I lay in my hospital bed, holding my beautiful baby girl, Sarah, my mind was already racing ahead to the future. I couldn't help but wonder what her life would be like, and more importantly, how she would compare to the other babies I saw on Instagram. Would she have the perfect button nose like little Emma? Would her eyes sparkle as brightly as Henry's? I couldn't wait to start documenting her journey, capturing every precious moment in perfect filters.

It seemed like a harmless obsession, at first. After all, who wouldn't want to showcase their little one's milestones and adorable moments to the world? In this age of social media, it has become almost second nature to share our lives with others, filtering our experiences to present a carefully perfect version of reality.

With each passing day, I would dive deeper into the world of filters. I studied the art of photography, learned about different editing techniques, and invested in top-of-the-line cameras and smartphones. I wanted nothing but the best to capture Sarah's life, to ensure she shone brighter than any other child on my social media feed.

It didn't take long for my once-innocent passion to turn into an obsession. I spent hours upon hours scrolling through parenting blogs and Instagram accounts, comparing Sarah's progress to others. Every little imperfection became a source of anxiety for me. If her first steps weren't as early as little

Sophia's, or if her first words didn't come as easily as Liam's, I felt a sense of failure as a parent. The pressure to be the best, to have the most enviable feed, was suffocating. I found myself fixated on the number of likes and comments my posts received, seeking validation from strangers behind glowing screens. It was a constant cycle of capturing the perfect moment, editing it to perfection, and then waiting anxiously for the world's approval.

When I first became a parent, I was filled with wonder and excitement. Holding Sarah in my arms for the first time was a magical experience. I wanted to document every milestone, every precious moment, and share it with the world. It started innocently enough, with a few posts here and there, capturing her adorable smile or her tiny hands reaching out for a toy. I reveled in the joy of motherhood and the ability to connect with other parents online.

But as time went on, my innocent passion for sharing turned into an unhealthy obsession. I became consumed by the need for validation and comparison. I would compare Sarah's achievements to other children's, constantly feeling like I was falling short. If a fellow mom shared a video of her child taking their first steps, I couldn't help but feel a pang of envy and disappointment. Why wasn't Sarah doing the same? Was there something wrong with her? I would spend endless nights researching developmental milestones, comparing her progress to other children her age. The weight of comparison was crushing, and it took a toll on my mental well-being.

Social media played a significant role in fueling my obsession. The endless stream of picture-perfect moments and seemingly flawless parenting created an unattainable standard. Every post I shared had to be carefully curated, edited to perfection. I would spend hours selecting the right filter, adjusting the brightness and saturation, desperate for my photos to fit the aesthetic of an enviable feed.

As the obsession grew, it started to impact my relationship with Sarah. Instead of being fully present in the moment, I would be preoccupied with capturing the perfect photo. I would rush her through experiences, eager to document them rather than savoring them together. Our special moments became photo opportunities, and the genuine connection between us started to fade.

One day, as I was scrolling through Instagram, I had a moment of clarity.

I realized that I had lost sight of what truly mattered. I had allowed the virtual world to dictate my self-worth as a parent and had neglected the real-life experiences and bond with Sarah. I made a conscious decision to step back from social media and reclaim my sanity.

It wasn't an easy journey. Breaking free from the obsession required a lot of self-reflection and self-compassion. I had to learn to embrace imperfection and let go of the need for external validation. I started focusing on the genuine joy and love I felt as a mother, rather than comparing myself to others.

Gradually, I began to find fulfillment in the little moments that didn't make it to social media. I relished in the sound of Sarah's laughter, the warmth of her tiny hand in mine, and the joy of watching her explore the world without the pressure of capturing it all for the online world.

I also sought support from fellow parents who understood the struggles and pressures of parenthood. I joined local parenting groups, attended support meetings, and engaged in meaningful conversations about the realities of raising children. Through these connections, I learned that every child develops at their own pace and that parenting is a journey unique to each individual.

Today, I am proud to say that I have found a healthier balance. I still appreciate the joy of sharing moments with others, but I no longer rely on it for validation. I prioritize being present for Sarah and cherishing the unfiltered, unedited moments we share together.

Parenthood is a beautiful and challenging journey, but it should not be defined by the standards of social media or the comparisons we make. It is about embracing the messy, imperfect reality and finding joy in the simple moments. My once-innocent passion may have turned into an unhealthy obsession, but through self-reflection and a shift in priorities, I have found my way back to the true essence of being a parent - love, connection, and unconditional acceptance.

But amidst this relentless pursuit of perfection, I began to lose sight of what truly mattered. The joy of witnessing Sarah's first giggle, her tiny fingers reaching out to explore the world around her, the warmth of her tiny body nestled against mine—they all became secondary to the never-ending quest for validation.

One day, as I set up yet another photoshoot to capture a perfectly staged moment, I noticed something remarkable. Sarah, who was now a year old, started giggling uncontrollably at the simplest of things—a fluttering butterfly, a bubble floating in the air. In that moment, I realized the immense beauty of authenticity.

I put down my camera and joined her in laughter, embracing the imperfect, unfiltered joy that only a child could bring. It was a turning point for me, a moment of clarity amidst the digital haze. From that day forward, I made a promise to myself and Sarah—I would no longer chase the illusion of perfection.

Instead, I would cherish every unfiltered, messy, and genuine moment we shared together. I would focus on being present, rather than obsessing over the perfect angle or the ideal filter. I would be her mother, her guiding light, her safe haven in a world that constantly demanded perfection.

With this new found resolve, I deleted my meticulously curated Instagram feed and started a new account, one that celebrated the beautiful chaos of parenthood. I shared unfiltered snapshots of our everyday life, capturing the genuine love and laughter that filled our days. And to my surprise, it resonated with others.

People were tired of the unrealistic expectations and unattainable standards. They longed for something real, something they could relate to. And in sharing my unfiltered journey, I found a community of parents who embraced imperfections and celebrated the beauty of authenticity.

As the years went by, Sarah grew up in a world where filters were just another tool, not a measure of worth or beauty. She learned to appreciate the unfiltered moments, the flaws that made her unique, and the love that bound our family together.

Looking back, I realized that the world of filters had nearly consumed me, threatening to overshadow the true essence of motherhood. But it was through that struggle that I discovered the real magic—the beauty that lies in embracing life, unfiltered and unapologetically imperfect.

And so, as I lay in bed once again, this time with my grown-up daughter by my side, I reflected on our incredible journey. The world had changed, and so had we. We had grown together, learned together, and found strength in each other's unfiltered presence.

As I closed my eyes, I whispered a silent prayer of gratitude. Gratitude for the journey, for the lessons learned, and for the unbreakable bond forged through the lens of authenticity. And as Sarah held my hand, I knew that we had truly captured the most precious moments, not in perfect filters, but in the depth of our hearts.

~ **Jane** ~

Chapter 2: The Quest for Perfection
"Lily and Noah"

With a smartphone in one hand and my baby, Lily, in the other, I delved into the world of social media. My Instagram feed became a constant source of inspiration and comparison. I scrolled endlessly, analyzing every photo, every smile, and every milestone. The pressure to present Lily as flawless was overwhelming, and I found myself spending hours searching for the perfect filter to enhance her beauty.

As I clicked through countless filters, each promising to magically transform ordinary moments into extraordinary ones, I couldn't help but wonder if I had fallen into a trap. Had I become so consumed with capturing the perfect image that I was missing out on truly experiencing the precious moments with Lily?

One day, as I sat in front of the screen, Lily cooing in my arms, I had an epiphany. It was as if a veil had been lifted, and I saw the world beyond the confines of social media. I realized that the quest for perfection had taken me away from the essence of life itself.

Determined to break free from the chains of comparison and superficiality, I made a decision. Lily and I would embark on a journey to discover the true meaning of beauty, unfiltered by the virtual world. We would learn to appreciate the imperfect moments, the messy hair, and the unfiltered emotions that make life so rich and meaningful.

Leaving my smartphone behind, I stepped outside and felt the warm embrace of the sun on my skin. With Lily in my arms, we strolled through the park, taking in the sights and sounds of nature. The vibrant colors of the flowers, the laughter of children playing, and the gentle rustle of leaves in the wind—all these simple pleasures seemed to come alive in a way they never had before.

As days turned into weeks, and weeks turned into months, I discovered a new found joy in the unedited moments of life. I reveled in the spontaneous laughter that erupted during tickle fights, the messy faces covered in chocolate from baking experiments, and the sleepy snuggles after a long day.

I realized that the true beauty of Lily lay not in perfectly edited photos but in her pure, unadulterated spirit. It was in the twinkle of her eyes when she discovered something new, the warmth of her tiny hand in mine, and the infectious giggles that echoed through our home.

I started capturing these moments with my heart instead of a lens. I didn't need filters to make them more beautiful; their authenticity radiated from within. I shared these experiences with friends and family, not to seek validation or likes, but to inspire them to embrace the unfiltered beauty in their own lives.

In this new found world, Lily flourished. She grew into a confident, compassionate, and resilient individual. She learned that life's true value lies in the relationships we build, the adventures we undertake, and the love we share—not in the number of followers or likes on a screen.

As Lily took her first steps into a world unfiltered by the constraints of social media, I realized that I, too, had grown. I had transformed from a person consumed by the quest for perfection to someone who appreciated the beauty in every imperfect moment.

And so, armed with the wisdom gained from our journey, I made a promise to myself and Lily. We would continue to navigate this world, not through the lens of filters and comparisons, but with open hearts and a genuine appreciation for the unfiltered beauty that surrounded us.

Together, we would rewrite the narrative of perfection and redefine what it truly means to live a meaningful life—one unfiltered moment at a time.

As I continued my journey of unfiltered parenting, I discovered a growing community of like-minded individuals who were also challenging the culture of perfection on social media. We bonded over shared experiences and encouraged each other to embrace authenticity in all aspects of our lives.

Together, we started a movement to promote genuine connections and meaningful interactions online. We encouraged parents to share unfiltered moments, to highlight the challenges and triumphs of parenting, and to support one another through the highs and lows. Our message resonated with many, and gradually, we saw a shift in the online landscape.

As Lily grew older, she developed a strong sense of self and an appreciation for authenticity. She understood that her worth didn't lie in the number of likes on a photo, but in her unique qualities and the love she shared with others. Together, we explored the world without the filter of societal expectations, embracing diversity and promoting kindness and acceptance.

Looking back, I realized that my initial fascination with perfection had stemmed from a desire to fit in, to be part of an idealized online world. But through my journey, I discovered that true connection and fulfillment come from embracing our true selves and celebrating the beauty of authenticity.

Now, as I cradle my grandchild, Noah, in my arms, I share the lessons I've learned with the next generation. I encourage my children and their children to navigate the online world with discernment, to value genuine connections over superficial validation, and to appreciate the unfiltered moments that make life rich and meaningful.

In this new era, the world of filters has transformed from a realm of superficiality to one that champions diversity, authenticity, and self-love. And as I watch Noah grow, I am hopeful that they will inherit a digital landscape where individuality is celebrated, where filters are used to amplify rather than disguise, and where the beauty of imperfection shines through.

As Noah grows older, they become an active participant in our movement for authenticity. Together, we organize events and workshops that promote self-expression, self-acceptance, and embracing one's unique qualities. We collaborate with artists, photographers, and influencers who share our vision, creating projects that celebrate diversity and challenge societal norms.

Noah, with his innate curiosity and open mind, becomes a catalyst for change within his own generation. He fearlessly shares his unfiltered stories, thoughts, and experiences, inspiring others to do the same. Through his influential voice, he encourages his peers to break free from the constraints of online perfection and to embrace the beauty of their authentic selves.

Through it all, I stand proud as a guiding force for my family. I witness the positive impact we've made and the lives we've touched through our commitment to authenticity. My heart swells with joy as I see Noah confidently navigate the online world, empowered to share his unfiltered truth and inspire others to do the same.

As I reflect on our journey, I am filled with gratitude for the lessons learned, the connections forged, and the legacy we've created. Together, we have rewritten the narrative of perfection and redefined what it means to live a meaningful life.

And so, with Noah by my side, I continue to champion authenticity, unfiltered beauty, and the power of embracing our true selves. We believe in a world where everyone is celebrated for their unique qualities and where the beauty of imperfection is embraced with open arms.

In this world, filters are seen as tools of creative expression rather than masks of conformity. The online sphere becomes a place of genuine connections, support, and inspiration. And as we navigate this digital landscape, we do so with open hearts, open minds, and an unwavering commitment to embracing the unfiltered beauty that resides within us all.

~ Sueann ~

Chapter 3: The Envy Trap "The Jealous momma"

As the months passed, I began to notice a gnawing sense of envy creeping into my heart. It seemed like every other mom had it all figured out. Their babies were always smiling, dressed in trendy clothes, and hitting milestones well ahead of schedule. Meanwhile, I struggled with sleepless nights, diaper blowouts, and the never-ending battle to capture that perfect moment.

It all started innocently enough. Scrolling through social media, I would come across picture-perfect images of blissful moms and their angelic babies. Their lives seemed like a highlight reel of joy and success, while mine felt like a series of clumsy missteps and messy mishaps. It was as if I was living in a parallel universe where everyone else had received a manual on perfect parenting, except me.

I couldn't help but compare myself to these seemingly flawless mothers. Their posts were carefully curated, capturing the ideal moments of motherhood, all filtered through a rose-colored lens. I found myself obsessing over their seemingly effortless success, wondering why I couldn't achieve the same level of perfection.

The envy crept into every aspect of my life. I envied the moms who managed to maintain their pre-pregnancy figures while I struggled to shed the baby weight. I envied the moms who effortlessly juggled their careers, social lives, and motherhood, while I felt like I was barely keeping my head above water. I envied the moms whose babies slept through the night, while mine seemed to be in a never-ending cycle of restlessness.

I was trapped in a never-ending cycle of comparison and self-doubt. Each time I saw a picture-perfect moment on my social media feed, my heart sank a little deeper. The envy took hold and whispered poisonous thoughts into my mind, telling me I was failing as a mother.

But as the months went by, I started to question the authenticity of these seemingly perfect lives. I began to wonder if what I saw on social media was just a carefully crafted facade, designed to elicit envy from others. Behind closed doors, were these moms struggling just like me? Were their babies crying through the night, refusing to eat, and throwing tantrums?

Determined to break free from the envy trap, I decided to reach out to other moms in my community. I joined a local parenting support group and attended playdates where I could connect with other mothers face-to-face. It was during these interactions that I realized I wasn't alone in my struggles.

As we sat together, sharing stories of sleepless nights and diaper disasters, I discovered that every mom faced challenges and moments of self-doubt. Behind the filters and carefully curated social media posts, we were all united by the messy, imperfect, and beautifully chaotic journey of motherhood.

One day, during a particularly low moment, I decided to peel back the glossy facade of Instagram and look beyond the filters. I reached out to a fellow mom, someone whose photos always seemed so picture-perfect. To my surprise, she confessed her own struggles and insecurities. We bonded over our shared experiences, realizing that the curated world of social media often hides the truth.

In those face-to-face conversations, I found solace and understanding. It became clear that the perfect images I saw on social media were just a tiny snapshot of a much bigger and messier reality. We shared stories of sleep deprivation, breastfeeding woes, and the endless cycle of laundry. We laughed together about the times we showed up to playdates with mismatched socks or baby spit-ups on our shoulders.

As I immersed myself in these genuine connections, I realized that motherhood wasn't about achieving perfection; it was about embracing imperfection and finding joy in the little moments. I learned that there was no one-size-fits-all approach to parenting and that each journey was unique.

Instead of comparing myself to other moms, I started celebrating my own victories, no matter how small they seemed. I celebrated the nights when my baby finally slept for a few hours straight or when I managed to get a nutritious meal on the table amidst the chaos. I discovered that motherhood was a journey of growth and learning, and it wasn't about reaching an unattainable standard of perfection.

Gradually, the envy that had once consumed me began to fade. I stopped obsessing over picture-perfect moments and started focusing on creating authentic memories with my child. I realized that the true beauty of motherhood lay in the messy, unfiltered moments—the late-night cuddles, the first giggles, and the milestones that were celebrated with imperfect but genuine joy.

Breaking free from the envy trap wasn't easy, and there were moments when I still found myself comparing. But whenever those feelings surfaced, I reminded myself of the connections I had made with other moms and the shared experiences we had. I reminded myself that I was doing the best I could, and that was enough.

As time went on, I discovered that the envy trap wasn't exclusive to motherhood. It was a trap that could ensnare us in various aspects of our lives, whether it was comparing careers, relationships, or personal achievements. The key was to shift the focus from comparison to self-acceptance and finding joy in our own journeys.

With this newfound perspective, I embraced motherhood wholeheartedly, cherishing both the triumphs and the challenges. I no longer saw other moms as rivals or competitors but as fellow warriors in this unpredictable adventure. We cheered each other on, offering support and encouragement along the way.

Motherhood became a tapestry woven with threads of love, resilience, and authenticity. And as I let go of the need for perfection, I discovered the true essence of being a mother—the unconditional love and unwavering dedication to nurturing and guiding another human being.

The envy trap could only hold me captive if I allowed it to. By seeking genuine connections, embracing imperfections, and celebrating my own unique journey, I found freedom and joy in motherhood. From that point forward, I vowed to live authentically and wholeheartedly, knowing that the messy moments were just as beautiful as the picture-perfect ones.

Gradually, I started to let go of the unrealistic expectations I had set for myself. I embraced the imperfections and embraced the messy moments. I realized that capturing the perfect moment wasn't as important as living it. The milestones my baby reached in their own time were more precious than any picture-perfect image.

I learned to celebrate the small victories, the tiny steps forward, and the love that overflowed from my heart. I understood that being a mom wasn't about having it all figured out but about being present, showing up, and cherishing the imperfect beauty of the journey.

The envy trap had consumed me for far too long, but now I saw the world through a different lens. I no longer compared my life to the carefully crafted images on social media. Instead, I focused on building genuine connections with other moms and finding solace in the shared experiences of motherhood.

As the months turned into years, my heart overflowed with gratitude. Gratitude for the messy moments, the diaper blowouts, and the sleepless nights. Gratitude for the lessons learned and the friendships forged. Most of all, gratitude for the joy and love that filled my life, despite the imperfections.

The envy trap had once threatened to suffocate me, but I had broken free. I had discovered that the real magic of motherhood wasn't found in picture-perfect images or envy-inducing posts. It was found in the messy, imperfect, and beautifully chaotic moments that were uniquely mine. And as I embraced the reality of my journey, I realized that I had it all figured out in my own imperfect way.

~ **Mary** ~

Chapter 4: The Social Media Comparison Game "Alex"

I sat on my couch, scrolling through my Instagram feed. As I swiped past perfectly staged family photos and meticulously edited vacation pictures, a familiar knot formed in my stomach. I couldn't help but compare my own life to the seemingly perfect lives of others.

My gaze shifted to a photo of my friend Sarah's son, Max, holding an impressive trophy from his school's science fair. Max's accomplishment filled the frame with pride and joy, and I couldn't help but feel a pang of envy. My own son, Alex, was talented in his own right, but his achievements were less flashy and Instagram-worthy.

My mind wandered to another post I had seen earlier that day. It was a video of Sarah's cousin's son, Ethan, scoring the winning goal in a soccer game. The comments section was filled with praise and admiration for Ethan's athletic prowess. I couldn't help but compare Ethan's success to Alex's less competitive interest in playing the piano. While I appreciated my son's dedication and musical talent, it often went unnoticed by others.

Frustration and self-doubt began to consume me. I wondered if I was doing enough as a mother. I started questioning my parenting decisions and choices, thinking that maybe I had somehow failed Alex. I felt the pressure to document every little achievement of my son's life to keep up with the relentless social media comparisons. The more I scrolled, the more I found myself in a whirlpool of self-doubt and inadequacy.

But then, as if waking from a trance, I paused. I looked up from my phone and glanced across the room where Alex was sitting, engrossed in a book. His eyes sparkled with curiosity and intelligence, and a gentle smile played on his lips. At that moment, I realized the trap I had fallen into.

I had allowed myself to get caught up in the highlight reels of other people's lives, comparing my own son to an idealized version of someone else's child. I had forgotten to appreciate and celebrate the unique qualities that made Alex who he was. His kindness, his empathy, and his love for learning were gifts that couldn't be measured by trophies or social media likes.

With new found clarity, I put my phone aside and walked over to Alex. I wrapped my arms around him, hugging him tightly. "You know what, Alex?" I said, my voice filled with love. "You are extraordinary just the way you are. Your talents and passions may not be the same as those we see online, but they are just as valuable."

Alex looked up at me, a mix of surprise and warmth in his eyes. He had always felt loved and supported, but in that moment, he felt a deep sense of appreciation for who he truly was.

From that day forward, I vowed to focus less on comparisons and more on nurturing my son's unique strengths. I would encourage him to explore his interests, embrace his passions, and celebrate his accomplishments, big or small, without the need for social media validation.

I had learned a valuable lesson about the dangers of the social media comparison game. I understood that every child is different, and true fulfillment as a parent comes from accepting and nurturing their individuality. And so, I embarked on a journey to be present, to love unconditionally, and to build my son's self-worth based on the things that truly mattered, beyond the shallow world of social media.

As I reflected on my journey as a parent, I realized that my own insecurities and the pressure to conform to societal expectations had influenced my perspective. I had been swept away by the illusion of perfection portrayed on social media, forgetting that life's true beauty lies in its imperfections.

I made a conscious effort to shift my focus towards fostering a loving and supportive environment for Alex. I encouraged him to pursue his passions and explore new interests without comparing himself to others. We spent more quality time together, engaging in meaningful conversations and activities that nourished his mind and spirit.

I also sought out communities and resources that celebrated individuality and diversity. I connected with other parents who shared similar experiences and learned from their wisdom. Surrounding myself with like-minded individuals who valued authenticity and genuine connections helped me find solace and reaffirm my belief in the power of nurturing a child's unique qualities.

Over time, I witnessed Alex blossom into a confident and self-assured individual. He began to embrace his own strengths and talents, unburdened by the need for external validation. We celebrated his accomplishments, big or small, within the confines of our home, where love and genuine pride filled the air.

Through this journey, I realized that social media could be a double-edged sword. While it provided a platform for connection and inspiration, it also had the potential to create unrealistic expectations and breed insecurity. I became more mindful of my own social media usage, recognizing the importance of maintaining a healthy balance and being discerning about the content I consumed.

As time went on, I became an advocate for promoting authenticity and self-acceptance in the realm of social media. I shared our story, highlighting the value of celebrating uniqueness and resisting the urge to compare. I hoped to inspire other parents to focus on nurturing their children's individuality and to find joy in the small moments that truly matter.

Ultimately, my experience taught me that being a parent is about guiding and supporting our children in discovering their own paths. It's about embracing their differences, celebrating their achievements, and fostering an environment where they can thrive as their authentic selves.

As I look back on that transformative period in my life, I am grateful for the lessons I learned and the bond that grew stronger between me and Alex. Together, we navigated the maze of social media comparisons and emerged with a new found appreciation for the beauty of individuality.

In our journey, I also learned to be kinder to myself. I realized that my worth as a parent was not determined by how my child measured up to others, but rather by the love, support, and guidance I provided. I gave myself permission to let go of unrealistic expectations and comparisons, focusing instead on creating a nurturing and accepting environment for Alex to flourish.

I encourage open communication with Alex, ensuring that he feels comfortable sharing his thoughts, dreams, and concerns with me. We celebrated his milestones and successes, not just on social media, but within the intimate moments we shared as a family. I made a conscious effort to listen attentively, to validate his emotions, and to provide guidance when needed.

As Alex grew older, I encouraged him to define his own measures of success and happiness. Together, we explored the importance of authenticity, resilience, and compassion. We emphasized the value of personal growth, embracing challenges as opportunities for learning and development.

I also made it a point to introduce Alex to a diverse range of experiences, cultures, and perspectives. By exposing him to different ways of life and encouraging empathy, I aimed to broaden his understanding of the world and foster acceptance and respect for others.

As the years passed, I witnessed Alex's self-confidence soar. He pursued his passions with unwavering dedication, unburdened by the need for external validation. I celebrated not only his achievements but also the person he had become—a kind-hearted, compassionate individual with a deep appreciation for the beauty of individuality.

Our journey taught me that parenting is a continuous process of growth and self-discovery. It's about creating a safe and nurturing space for our children to explore their identities and embrace their unique gifts. It's about recognizing that each child has their own journey and that true fulfillment comes from supporting them in becoming the best version of themselves.

Through the highs and lows, I remained committed to the lessons I had learned. I became an advocate for mindful parenting, promoting the celebration of individuality, and resisting the pitfalls of social media comparisons. I shared my experiences, not to boast or seek validation, but to inspire others to focus on what truly matters—the well-being and happiness of our children.

Today, as I reflect on our journey, I am filled with pride and gratitude. I see Alex flourishing in his pursuits, confident in his own skin, and embracing the unique path he is carving for himself. And I am reminded, once again, that being a parent is not about molding our children to fit societal standards but about empowering them to embrace their authentic selves.

In the end, our worth as parents lies not in the number of likes or accolades our children receive, but in the love, guidance, and acceptance we provide. And as I continue to navigate the ever-evolving landscape of parenthood, I do so with a deep sense of purpose—to cultivate an environment where my child can thrive, shine, and embrace the extraordinary person he is meant to be.

As the years passed, I witnessed the positive impact of our parenting approach on Alex's overall well-being and happiness. He continued to pursue his passions with enthusiasm and resilience, unswayed by the pressures of comparison. Together, we celebrated his triumphs and milestones, big or small, acknowledging the effort and dedication he put into his endeavors.

I also made sure to provide a balanced perspective on social media. We had open discussions about its curated nature and the importance of distinguishing reality from the highlight reels presented online. I encouraged Alex to engage with social media mindfully, using it as a tool for inspiration rather than a yardstick for self-worth.

In our household, we prioritized fostering strong values such as kindness, empathy, and gratitude. We engaged in acts of service and volunteered in our community, teaching Alex the importance of giving back and making a positive difference in the lives of others. By instilling these core values, I hoped to equip him with a solid foundation for a fulfilling and purposeful life.

As Alex entered his teenage years, I recognized the significance of granting him increasing autonomy and independence. I encouraged him to explore his own identity, make decisions, and learn from the consequences of his choices. I became his trusted confidante, providing guidance and support while also respecting his individuality and personal growth.

Throughout our journey, I never stopped learning. I sought out resources, books, and workshops on positive parenting, adolescent development, and fostering resilience. I connected with other parents who shared similar philosophies, exchanging insights and experiences that enriched our own parenting practices.

As Alex approached adulthood, I marveled at the confident and compassionate person he had become. His unique strengths and perspectives shone brightly, and I couldn't be prouder of the young adult he had evolved into. Our journey together had taught me invaluable lessons about embracing individuality, letting go of comparison, and nurturing the true essence of a person.

Looking back, I realized that our path had not been without its challenges. There were moments of doubt, set-backs, and uncertainties. But it was through those experiences that we both grew stronger and more resilient. We weathered the storms together, with unwavering love and support as our guiding force.

As Alex set out to forge his own path in the world, I remained a steadfast pillar of support. I cheered him on from the sidelines, reminding him that success is not measured solely by societal standards but by the happiness, fulfillment, and authenticity he found along the way.

Our journey as parent and child will continue to evolve, and I am excited for what the future holds. I am grateful for the opportunity to witness Alex's continued growth and to be a part of his remarkable journey of self-discovery. And in the depths of my heart, I know that the lessons we learned together will forever guide me as a parent, shaping the way I nurture and support not only my own child but also the beautiful souls I encounter along the way.

As Alex embarked on his own path, I found solace in knowing that our journey together had laid a strong foundation for him to navigate life's challenges with resilience and authenticity. We maintained a deep bond, built on trust and unconditional love, as I continued to be his unwavering source of support and guidance.

I encouraged Alex to pursue his dreams fearlessly, reminding him that success is not a linear path but a culmination of perseverance, passion, and personal fulfillment. We explored various opportunities for growth, whether it be through internships, mentorships, or engaging in meaningful projects aligned with his interests.

During this phase, I also emphasized the importance of self-care and mental well-being. We had open conversations about managing stress, setting boundaries, and practicing self-compassion. Together, we explored mindfulness techniques, exercise routines, and healthy coping strategies that would serve him well throughout his life.

As Alex flourished in his endeavors, I was reminded once again of the immense joy and pride that come from embracing and celebrating individuality. I witnessed his impact on others, as his unique perspectives and talents enriched the lives of those around him. It was a testament to the power of embracing one's authentic self and finding fulfillment beyond the superficial measurements of success.

Our journey together extended beyond the boundaries of our immediate family. We actively sought out communities and organizations that shared our values, creating a network of like-minded individuals who celebrated diversity, kindness, and personal growth. Through these connections, Alex found mentors, friends, and role models who further inspired and supported his journey.

As time went on, I embraced the role of a lifelong learner, recognizing that parenting is an ever-evolving process. I sought out wisdom from those who had traversed similar paths, embracing their insights while staying true to our family's values and dynamics. I remained open to new ideas, perspectives, and approaches, always striving to create an environment that nurtured Alex's evolving needs and aspirations.

Now, as Alex steps into adulthood, I look back at our journey with profound gratitude. Together, we had shattered the confines of comparison and societal expectations, paving the way for a future rooted in self-acceptance, resilience, and purpose. Our bond remained unbreakable, as I continue to be his biggest cheerleader and confidante, offering guidance whenever he seeks it.

In the grand tapestry of parenthood, I have come to understand that it is not a destination but an ongoing voyage of love, growth, and self-discovery. Our journey was marked by beautiful moments of celebration, but also by challenges that tested our resolve. Yet, through it all, we emerged stronger and more connected.

As I look forward to what lies ahead, I am filled with hope and anticipation. I know that Alex will continue to make a positive impact in the world, bringing his unique gifts and perspectives to every endeavor he undertakes. And I am grateful for the privilege of being his parent, witnessing the unfolding of his potential and sharing in the joy of his triumphs.

Our journey is a testament to the transformative power of embracing individuality and celebrating the extraordinary qualities that make each person unique. It is a reminder that true fulfillment as a parent lies not in comparison or external validation, but in nurturing the growth and happiness of our children as they forge their own paths and become the incredible individuals they were meant to be.

~ **Vanessa** ~

Chapter 5: Behind the Screens "The real deal"

One day, during a particularly low moment, I decided to peel back the glossy facade of Instagram and look beyond the filters. I reached out to a fellow mom, someone whose photos always seemed so picture-perfect. To my surprise, she confessed her own struggles and insecurities. We bonded over our shared experiences, realizing that the curated world of social media often hides the truth.

In the digital realm, where moments are captured and shared at lightning speed, mothers found solace in the virtual world. Social media platforms became their stages, and their babies, the stars of the show. It was a realm where love and pride for their little ones knew no bounds, but it also became a battlefield for comparison, judgment, and the ever-persistent quest for validation.

Scrolling through their feeds, mothers encountered a colorful mosaic of precious snapshots. The realm of social media had become an endless parade of milestone achievements, from the first toothy grin to the wobbly steps of their offspring. It was a place where time stood still, and every accomplishment was amplified. Yet, amidst the sea of adorable baby pictures, an unspoken competition began to emerge.

Mothers found themselves unwittingly drawn into a whirlwind of comparisons. The age at which each baby achieved certain milestones became a measure of success, and each development seemed to carry the weight of an unspoken challenge. Conversations shifted from genuine exchanges of joy and support to carefully crafted narratives designed to outshine others.

One mother would share a video of her little one taking their first steps, and within seconds, another mother would swoop in with a more impressive display—her baby effortlessly balancing on one foot while juggling toys. The cycle continued, spiraling into a never-ending cycle of one-upmanship. It seemed that every milestone was an opportunity for mothers to stake their claim on the social media pedestal.

Behind the scenes, however, a different story unfolded. Late-night feeds, sleepless nights, and the ever-chaotic world of parenthood were never captured in these curated moments. The struggles and challenges faced by each mother were shielded from the public eye, hidden beneath filters and carefully selected captions.

As the obsession with comparison grew, so did the burden on these mothers. Doubt crept in, clouding their sense of joy and accomplishment. Was their baby progressing fast enough? Were they failing as a parent if their little one fell behind the imaginary curve? In their quest to keep up, the essence of motherhood often became overshadowed, obscured by the pursuit of online validation.

Deep down, every mother knew that the true worth of their child could never be measured by arbitrary milestones or online likes. The purity of a mother's love transcended the digital realm, embracing the imperfections and unique journey of each little one. But in the face of societal pressure and the constant barrage of social media comparisons, it became increasingly difficult to hold onto this truth.

It was time for a shift—a collective awakening. Mothers began to reclaim the joy and authenticity of motherhood, away from the constraints of social media's measuring tape. They formed communities that celebrated diversity, empathy, and the shared experiences of raising children. They reminded each other that there was no race to win or crown to claim, only the precious moments to be treasured and cherished.

And so, gradually, the focus shifted from comparing babies to celebrating them. Mothers discovered the power of genuine connection, support, and solidarity, finding solace in the understanding that motherhood was not a competition but a collective journey. The social media battleground became a place of nurturing, empowering, and uplifting one another, one shared moment at a time.

The babies, blissfully unaware of the online frenzy, continued to grow and thrive in the arms of their loving mothers, basking in the warmth of unconditional love. And in this newfound equilibrium, the true beauty of motherhood was allowed to shine, unfettered by the virtual spotlight.

Amidst the noise of comparison and the quest for validation, a movement began to take shape within the realm of social media. Mothers, weary of the artificial pressures and endless competition, sought to redefine their online presence and reclaim their authenticity.

In a world saturated with perfectly curated feeds and glossy portrayals of motherhood, a group of brave women dared to defy the norms. They embraced imperfections, shared raw moments, and celebrated the messy, unfiltered reality of raising children. The movement was a rebellion against the polished facade and a celebration of the genuine bonds formed between mothers and their babies.

Through heartfelt posts, vulnerable confessions, and unedited glimpses into their daily lives, these mothers created a space where others felt seen and understood. They shattered the illusion that motherhood was flawless and unattainable, instead embracing the beautifully imperfect nature of the journey.

No longer did mothers feel the need to present themselves as super woman who effortlessly juggled it all. They found solace in sharing their struggles, fears, and insecurities, discovering a supportive community that offered empathy and encouragement. The virtual stage transformed into a safe haven—a place where vulnerability was not a weakness, but a strength.

In this new era of authenticity, the focus shifted from comparison to connection. Mothers started engaging in meaningful conversations, offering advice, and lending a sympathetic ear to those in need. The community became a lifeline—a source of support and understanding that transcended the boundaries of the digital world.

The images that once portrayed perfect babies with flawless smiles were now joined by snapshots of tantrums, messy meal times, and tear-stained faces. These images were not meant to capture picture-perfect moments, but to encapsulate the reality of motherhood in all its beautiful chaos. And with each shared experience, mothers realized they were not alone in their struggles.

As the movement gained momentum, society's perception of motherhood began to shift. The pressure to conform to an unattainable standard was replaced by an appreciation for the diversity and individuality of each mother and her child. The notion that every baby followed a predetermined timeline of achievements crumbled, making room for the recognition that every child's journey was unique and should be celebrated as such.

Mothers no longer sought external validation but drew strength from within. They found joy in their child's laughter, comfort in the warmth of tiny arms wrapped around them, and pride in the love they shared. The online world became a tool to connect and uplift rather than a battleground for comparison.

In the midst of this transformation, mothers discovered a new found sense of self. They embraced their imperfections, released themselves from the shackles of judgment, and redefined their own paths as mothers. No longer burdened by the need to prove themselves, they found freedom in embracing their own truths.

The movement of authenticity grew, sweeping across social media like a gentle breeze, reminding mothers everywhere of their inherent worth and the immeasurable value of their love. It was a reminder that no comparison could capture the magic that unfolded within the heart of a mother.

And so, with each shared post, heartfelt comment, and virtual hug, the community of mothers flourished. Authenticity became their armor, empowering them to rise above the noise and embrace the beauty of their own unique stories. In this new found space of love, acceptance, and connection, they found the strength to nurture not only their babies but also themselves.

Motherhood, once a landscape of fierce competition, had transformed into a garden of collective growth, where authenticity bloomed, and love thrived. And as mothers continued to navigate the ever-changing world of social media, they held steadfast to the knowledge that their worth was not defined by likes or followers, but by the immeasurable love they poured into their precious children.

~ Empowered Mothers ~

Chapter 6: Rediscovering Authenticity "Jane's Story"

As a mother, I began questioning the purpose and impact of my social media obsession. I couldn't help but wonder if constantly comparing myself to others was truly bringing me joy or if it was causing unnecessary stress. I realized that I had lost sight of the unfiltered beauty in the everyday moments—the messy hair, the giggles, and the pure joy of being a mom. It was time for me to take a step back and reevaluate my relationship with social media.

I made the decision to take a break from social media and embarked on a personal experiment to see how it would affect my overall well-being. At first, it was difficult to resist the urge to check notifications and mindlessly scroll through endless feeds. However, as days turned into weeks, I started noticing positive changes in myself.

Without the constant pressure to portray a perfect life online, I felt a weight lifted off my shoulders. I no longer had to worry about capturing the picture-perfect moments or crafting witty captions to impress others. Instead, I could fully immerse myself in the present, cherishing the genuine experiences without seeking validation from virtual strangers.

During this social media hiatus, I had more time for self-reflection and introspection. I realized that my self-worth should not be tied to likes, comments, or follower counts. My value as a person and as a mother lies in my unique qualities, my relationships, and the impact I have on the people around me.

Without the constant comparisons, my self-esteem began to flourish. I focused on nurturing my passions, exploring new hobbies, and connecting with loved ones on a deeper level. Instead of mindlessly scrolling, I read books, went for long walks in nature, and engaged in meaningful conversations. I discovered the joy of being fully present in my life, unburdened by the pressure to document and share every moment.

As time went on, I realized that I could still use social media as a tool for connection and inspiration, but with a healthier mindset. I reevaluated my social media usage and set boundaries that allowed me to engage with it consciously and intentionally. I became more selective about the content I consumed, following accounts that aligned with my values and interests, and unfollowing those that triggered negative emotions or unhealthy comparisons.

When I eventually returned to social media, I did so with a newfound perspective. I shared my journey of self-discovery and the lessons I had learned. I opened up about the challenges of balancing authenticity and the desire for validation, encouraging others to reflect on their own relationships with social media.

Ultimately, my break from social media helped me understand the importance of finding a balance between the virtual world and the real world. I now use social media as a platform for genuine connection, sharing meaningful moments, and uplifting others rather than seeking external validation or comparing myself to an idealized version of others. Rediscovering authenticity has brought me a sense of inner peace and contentment, allowing me to embrace the unfiltered beauty of my life and appreciate the joy of being true to myself.

In this journey of rediscovery, I've learned that motherhood is not about striving for perfection or conforming to societal expectations. It's about embracing the messy, imperfect, and authentic moments that make it uniquely beautiful. By embracing my own authenticity, I can create a loving and nurturing environment for my child, where they can grow and thrive while being their true selves.

Through this experience, I hope to inspire other mothers to question their own relationship with social media and rediscover the true beauty of motherhood. I encourage them to take a step back, reflect on what truly brings them joy, and embrace the unfiltered moments that make their journey as a mother extraordinary. Together, we can create a supportive community that celebrates authenticity, vulnerability, and the imperfectly perfect moments of motherhood

As I continued on my journey of rediscovering authenticity, I found that it had a profound impact on my overall well-being as a mother. By letting go of the need for validation and comparison, I was able to fully embrace the unique experience of raising my child. I no longer felt the pressure to conform to societal standards or portray a perfect image.

Instead, I focused on creating a loving and supportive environment where my child could grow and thrive, guided by the authenticity and unconditional love that I now embodied.

Through my own self-acceptance and authenticity, I hoped to instill in my child a sense of confidence and the courage to embrace their own individuality. I wanted them to grow up knowing that they didn't need to compare themselves to others or seek validation from external sources. Their worth would always come from within, and their true beauty would shine through in the unfiltered moments of their lives.

As I reentered the world of social media, I approached it with a renewed purpose. I used it as a platform to share my genuine experiences, to uplift and inspire other mothers, and to foster meaningful connections. Instead of focusing on the number of likes or followers, I prioritized the quality of the interactions and the impact I could have on others. I shared not only the joys and triumphs of motherhood but also the struggles and challenges, knowing that vulnerability could create a space for empathy, understanding, and support.

Rediscovering authenticity also meant being mindful of the boundaries I set in my online interactions. I ensured that I allocated quality time for my child and loved ones, free from the distractions of social media. I established specific times to engage with it consciously, avoiding mindless scrolling and the comparison trap. By prioritizing the present moment, I could fully immerse myself in the unfiltered beauty of my life, cherishing the fleeting moments that motherhood offers.

Through my journey, I have come to understand that authenticity is an ongoing process—a continuous exploration of self-discovery and growth. It requires constant reflection, reassessment, and realignment with my core values. There are days when I may still feel the pull of comparison or the need for validation, but I now possess the tools and mindset to navigate those challenges with grace and self-compassion.

As a mother, I encourage fellow moms to embark on their own journey of rediscovering authenticity. Let go of the pressures and expectations imposed by society or social media. Embrace the messy, imperfect, and unfiltered moments that make your journey as a mother uniquely yours. Cherish the joy, the love, and the connection that exist beyond the screens and the curated images. Find solace and strength in your authentic self, knowing that you are enough and that your journey as a mother is a true testament to your resilience, love, and devotion.

Together, as we embrace authenticity and empower one another, we can reshape the narrative of motherhood. We can celebrate the beauty of the unfiltered moments, the messy hair, the imperfections, and the genuine connections. And in doing so, we can inspire future generations of mothers to value their own authenticity and create a world where the true essence of motherhood is cherished and celebrated.

As I delved deeper into my journey of rediscovering authenticity, I found that it had a profound impact not only on myself but also on my relationships with others. By embracing my true self and letting go of the need for validation, I created a space for more genuine and meaningful connections.

I began to prioritize quality time with my loved ones, fully present and engaged in the moment. Instead of being distracted by the virtual world, I focused on fostering deeper connections with my child, partner, family, and friends. I savored the unfiltered moments of laughter, shared experiences, and heartfelt conversations. I discovered that true connection and fulfillment come from being present, attentive, and vulnerable in our relationships.

Moreover, my journey of authenticity allowed me to become a source of inspiration and support for other mothers. As I shared my challenges, triumphs, and lessons learned, I received an outpouring of encouragement and gratitude from fellow moms who resonated with my experiences. Together, we created a community that celebrated authenticity, vulnerability, and the shared joys and struggles of motherhood.

In this community, we uplifted one another, offering a safe space for validation, understanding, and empathy. We celebrated the beauty in each other's unfiltered moments, reminding ourselves that perfection is not the goal, but rather embracing our unique journeys and supporting one another through the ups and downs.

I also found that my journey of authenticity had a positive impact on my child. By embracing my true self and showing them that it's okay to be imperfect and vulnerable, I was able to cultivate an environment of acceptance and self-love. My child learned that their worth was not tied to external validation or societal expectations but was rooted in their own unique qualities and the love they received unconditionally.

As a mother, I am now more attuned to the importance of modeling authenticity and self-acceptance for my child. I encourage them to embrace their individuality, to celebrate their strengths, and to embrace their flaws as opportunities for growth and learning. I want them to know that their authentic self is worthy of love and respect, and that being true to themselves is a source of strength and empowerment.

In the process of rediscovering authenticity, I have come to appreciate the unfiltered beauty in every aspect of motherhood. From the messy hair and sleepless nights to the spontaneous moments of joy and the profound love that fills my heart, I have learned to embrace it all. I now find joy in the unscripted moments, knowing that they are the essence of what it means to be a mother.

Through my journey, I have realized that authenticity is not a destination but a continuous evolution. It requires ongoing self-reflection, self-compassion, and a commitment to living in alignment with our true selves. It's about embracing the messy, imperfect, and unfiltered aspects of our lives and finding beauty and strength within them.

As I continue to grow and navigate the ever-changing landscape of motherhood, I hold onto the lessons I have learned on this journey of rediscovering authenticity. I celebrate the unfiltered beauty of motherhood, cherishing the genuine connections, the growth, and the love that fill my days. And I invite every mother to embark on their own path of authenticity, to embrace the unfiltered moments, and to find solace and strength in being true to themselves.

As I reflect further on my journey of rediscovering authenticity as a mother, I realize that it has influenced not only my personal life but also the way I approach parenting and the values I instill in my child.

By embracing authenticity, I have shifted my focus from external validation to cultivating internal resilience and self-belief in my child. I encourage them to be true to themselves, to express their thoughts and emotions openly, and to embrace their own unique qualities and talents. I emphasize the importance of self-acceptance, teaching them that their worth is not determined by the opinions of others but by their own self-perception and the values they hold dear.

In this age of social media and constant comparison, it is crucial for me as a mother to guide my child in understanding that the glossy, filtered images they see online are just fragments of reality. I teach them to discern between the curated narratives presented on social media and the authentic experiences and connections that truly matter in life.

I have become more intentional in cultivating a balanced relationship with technology and social media for my child. I encourage them to use these platforms as tools for connection, learning, and creativity, rather than sources of validation or self-worth. Together, we explore the importance of setting boundaries and practicing mindful engagement in the digital realm, ensuring that it doesn't overshadow the genuine connections and experiences that exist offline.

Through my journey of authenticity, I have also become an advocate for mindful parenting. I prioritize active listening, open communication, and fostering a non-judgmental space for my child to express themselves. I strive to create an environment where they feel safe to embrace their true selves, ask questions, and make mistakes without fear of judgment or rejection.

I understand that authenticity is not about being perfect or having all the answers as a parent. It is about being genuine, vulnerable, and willing to learn and grow alongside my child. I embrace the opportunity to share my own imperfections and life lessons, encouraging them to learn from both my successes and failures. By doing so, I hope to teach them the value of resilience, self-reflection, and the beauty of embracing authenticity in all areas of their lives.

As I continue on this journey, I am grateful for the newfound sense of fulfillment and contentment that comes with embracing authenticity as a mother. I celebrate the unfiltered beauty of the messy, imperfect, and genuine moments of motherhood, knowing that it is within these moments that the true essence of parenting resides.

I encourage all mothers to embark on their own path of rediscovering authenticity, knowing that it is through embracing our true selves that we can create a nurturing, loving, and empowering environment for our children. Let us prioritize the unfiltered moments, the genuine connections, and the values that truly matter, shaping the future generation with the power of authenticity and genuine love.

~ **Jane** ~

Chapter 7: Embracing Imperfections "The Triumphant mom"

No longer bound by the need to compare, I found freedom in embracing the imperfections. I learned to celebrate my baby's uniqueness and appreciate her journey, no matter how it differed from others. I realized that being a mom wasn't about conforming to an ideal but rather about nurturing and cherishing the tiny soul entrusted to my care.

Embracing imperfections has transformed my perspective on motherhood. No longer burdened by societal expectations or the pressure to achieve some elusive standard of perfection, I have discovered a new found sense of freedom and contentment. In releasing the need to compare my journey as a mother with others, I have unlocked the ability to fully appreciate and celebrate my baby's uniqueness.

Each child is a distinct individual with their own set of strengths, weaknesses, and quirks. Through embracing imperfections, I have come to understand that these differences are not flaws to be corrected but rather aspects to be cherished. My baby's journey may deviate from the conventional norms, but it is in these divergences that her true essence and beauty are revealed.

Motherhood is a deeply personal and intimate experience. It is a journey of growth, both for the child and for the mother. By accepting imperfections, I have been able to let go of unrealistic expectations and embrace the messy, unpredictable nature of parenting. Rather than striving for an unattainable ideal, I have shifted my focus to nurturing and cherishing the tiny soul entrusted to my care.

In celebrating imperfections, I have also discovered a profound sense of self-acceptance and self-compassion. I have learned to acknowledge my own limitations and embrace the fact that I, too, am a work in progress. Through my baby's journey, I have witnessed the power of resilience and adaptability, and it has inspired me to embrace those qualities within myself.

Embracing imperfections has allowed me to cultivate a more authentic and fulfilling relationship with my child. Instead of trying to mold her into someone she is not, I am committed to providing a safe and nurturing environment that supports her individuality. I have learned to trust in her innate abilities and to encourage her to explore and discover the world in her own unique way.

In a society that often emphasizes achievement and conformity, embracing imperfections is a radical act of rebellion. It is a deliberate choice to reject unrealistic standards and to embrace the messy, imperfect reality of life. By doing so, we not only find freedom and joy in our own journeys but also pave the way for our children to grow into confident and resilient individuals who are unafraid to embrace their own imperfections.

Embracing imperfections in motherhood has taught me that the beauty of life lies in its impermanence, unpredictability, and uniqueness. It is through embracing these imperfections that we find the true essence of love, growth, and connection. Embracing imperfections extends beyond the realm of motherhood and seeps into every aspect of my life. It has become a guiding principle that allows me to navigate the complexities and challenges that arise on a daily basis.

In a world that often values perfection and polished appearances, embracing imperfections is a radical act of self-acceptance. It means embracing the scars and blemishes, both physical and emotional, that make us who we are. It means recognizing that our flaws and mistakes are an integral part of our humanity and that they do not define our worth.

By embracing imperfections, I have learned to approach life with a sense of curiosity and openness. I have let go of the fear of failure and instead view mistakes as valuable learning opportunities. I no longer strive for an unattainable ideal of perfection but rather focus on growth, progress, and self-improvement.

Embracing imperfections has also allowed me to cultivate deeper connections and relationships with others. When we let go of the need to project an image of flawlessness, we create space for authenticity and vulnerability. By sharing our imperfections, we invite others to do the same, fostering a sense of empathy and understanding.

In embracing imperfections, I have come to appreciate the beauty in the imperfect moments of life. The spontaneous laughter, the messy adventures, and the unexpected detours all contribute to the rich tapestry of our experiences. It is through these imperfect moments that we often find the most genuine joy and meaning.

Furthermore, embracing imperfections has taught me the importance of self-compassion. Instead of being overly critical of myself for not meeting unrealistic expectations, I practice kindness and understanding. I acknowledge that I am a complex and evolving individual, and that missteps and set-backs are a natural part of the journey.

Embracing imperfections is not about complacency or settling for mediocrity. It is about recognizing that perfection is an illusion and that true growth and fulfillment come from embracing the messy and imperfect parts of ourselves and our lives. It is about striving for progress rather than perfection, and finding beauty and strength in our unique journeys.

As I continue to embrace imperfections, I find myself liberated from the shackles of self-judgment and comparison. I am more present in each moment, fully accepting of myself and others as we are. I am able to embrace the uncertainties and challenges that life presents, knowing that imperfections are not obstacles but rather opportunities for growth and self-discovery.

Embracing imperfections is an ongoing process, a daily practice that requires self-awareness, compassion, and a willingness to let go of societal expectations. It is a journey towards self-acceptance, resilience, and authenticity. By embracing imperfections, we can truly embrace the beauty of being mothers.

Embracing imperfections has opened up a world of creativity and innovation in my life. By letting go of the pressure to be perfect, I have given myself permission to explore new ideas, take risks, and make mistakes along the way. It is through these imperfections that I have discovered unique solutions and uncovered hidden talents within myself.

In embracing imperfections, I have also developed a greater sense of resilience. Life is filled with ups and downs, challenges and set-backs. By accepting that imperfections are a natural part of the journey, I have learned to bounce back from failures and set-backs with renewed determination. I no longer view mistakes as reasons to give up, but rather as stepping stones towards growth and improvement as a mom.

Moreover, embracing imperfections has allowed me to develop a more compassionate and empathetic mindset. When I acknowledge and accept my own imperfections, it becomes easier to extend the same understanding to others. I recognize that everyone is on their own unique path, facing their own struggles and imperfections. This realization fosters a sense of connection and encourages me to support and uplift other moms in their journeys.

Embracing imperfections has also shifted my perspective on success. Rather than defining success solely by external achievements or societal standards, I now measure success by personal growth, fulfillment, and the positive impact I can have on others. It is through embracing imperfections that I have found a deeper sense of purpose and authenticity in my endeavors.

In a world that often values superficial appearances and instant gratification, embracing imperfections is a powerful act of self-love and self-acceptance. It allows us to break free from the limitations of perfectionism and embrace our true selves, with all our flaws and strengths.

By embracing imperfections, we embrace the beauty of the messy, imperfect, and ever-evolving nature of life itself. We recognize that life is not meant to be perfect, but rather a journey filled with growth, learning, and self-discovery. It is through embracing imperfections that we find the courage to step outside our comfort zones, embrace our true potential, and live a life that is uniquely our own.

So let us continue to embrace imperfections in all areas of our lives, be it in our relationships, our work, or our personal growth. Let us celebrate the beauty in the imperfect moments, the lessons learned from mistakes, and the growth that comes from embracing our true selves. Embracing imperfections is an ongoing journey, but it is one that leads us to a life filled with authenticity, resilience, and joy.

In a world saturated with social media and a constant barrage of curated perfection, it's easy to get caught up in the pursuit of an idealized version of motherhood. The pressure to showcase our lives in the best light often leads us to compare our babies and ourselves to others, as if happiness can be measured in likes and comments. But as I've come to realize, true joy in motherhood isn't found in the virtual realm—it's found in the real, unfiltered moments.

When I let go of the need to document and compare every aspect of my baby's life, I discovered a newfound appreciation for the messy, unpredictable beauty of the present. It's in those messy faces after mealtime, with food smeared across chubby cheeks and a mischievous glimmer in her eyes, that I find joy. It's in the belly laughs that fill the room during playtime, where time seems to stand still and the world is filled with pure happiness. And it's in the sleepy snuggles in the twilight hours, when the world is quiet and it's just the two of us, that I feel an overwhelming sense of love and contentment.

These are the moments that matter, the moments that create lasting memories and forge an unbreakable bond between a mother and her child. They are not captured in carefully curated photos or filtered through the lens of comparison. Instead, they are experienced fully and wholeheartedly, with all the imperfections and spontaneity that make them real.

My baby is a unique individual, with her own quirks, strengths, and personality. She doesn't need the validation of social media or the unrealistic standards set by others to shine. In her innocence and authenticity, she is perfect just the way she is. And as her mother, I am privileged to witness and nurture her growth, to guide her through life's ups and downs, and to love her unconditionally.

Finding joy in the real means embracing the imperfect, messy, and sometimes chaotic aspects of motherhood. It means letting go of the need for external validation and finding fulfillment in the genuine moments that unfold naturally. It's about treasuring the small victories, the everyday miracles, and the simple pleasures that bring us closer to our children and remind us of what truly matters.

So, I choose to savor the real moments—the ones that can't be captured in a photograph or measured by societal standards. I choose to celebrate the unique journey of motherhood, with all its challenges and joys. And in doing so, I find a deeper and more profound joy that fills my heart and nourishes my soul.

In my quest to find joy in the real, I've also learned the importance of being present in each moment with my baby. It's easy to get caught up in the distractions of daily life, constantly multitasking and worrying about what's next on the to-do list. But when I consciously choose to be fully present with my child, I discover a whole new level of joy and connection.

Being present means setting aside distractions, putting away the phone, and truly engaging with my baby. It means giving her my undivided attention, listening to her babbling with genuine interest, and responding to her cues and needs. It means immersing myself in the simple pleasure of watching her explore the world around her, marveling at her curiosity and the wonder in her eyes.

In those moments of presence, I am able to truly appreciate the beauty of my baby's growth and development. I witness the milestones, both big and small, and celebrate her achievements with genuine excitement. I find joy in the little victories, like when she takes her first wobbly steps or utters her first words. And even in the challenging moments, like when she's fussy or teething, I remind myself to stay present and offer comfort and reassurance.

Through presence, I also cultivate a deep sense of gratitude for the privilege of being a mother. I am grateful for the opportunity to witness the miracle of life unfolding before my eyes, to be entrusted with the responsibility of nurturing and shaping another human being. I am grateful for the lessons my baby teaches me about patience, resilience, and unconditional love. And I am grateful for the moments of pure joy and connection that fill my heart and remind me of the profound purpose and meaning motherhood brings to my life.

Finding joy in the real is an ongoing journey, one that requires conscious effort and a shift in mindset. It's about embracing the imperfections, staying present in the moment, and cherishing the genuine connections that motherhood brings. It's about recognizing that true joy lies not in comparison or external validation, but in the authentic experiences and emotions we share with our children.

As I continue to navigate the beautiful chaos of motherhood, I am committed to finding joy in the real, celebrating the unique and imperfect moments that make up our lives. I am determined to create a legacy of love, laughter, and cherished memories for my baby, knowing that true joy can be found in the simplest and most genuine moments we share together.

In my pursuit of finding joy in the real, I have also discovered the power of self-care and the importance of nurturing my own well-being as a mother. It is all too easy to get lost in the demands of motherhood, constantly putting our needs on the back burner. However, I've come to realize that taking care of myself is not a selfish act but a necessary one for both my own happiness and my ability to be a present and loving mother.

Self-care looks different for everyone, but for me, it involves finding moments of solitude and self-reflection amidst the busyness of daily life. It might be as simple as stealing a few minutes in the morning to enjoy a cup of tea and gather my thoughts before the chaos ensues. It could be indulging in a long, relaxing bath after my baby has fallen asleep, allowing myself to unwind and recharge. It might also involve pursuing hobbies or interests that bring me joy and a sense of fulfillment, whether it's reading, painting, or practicing yoga.

By prioritizing self-care, I replenish my own energy reserves and cultivate a sense of inner calm. This, in turn, allows me to show up as a more patient, compassionate, and present mother. When I take care of myself, I am better equipped to handle the challenges that motherhood presents, and I am able to give my baby the love and attention she deserves.

Moreover, self-care extends beyond individual activities. It also involves reaching out for support and building a network of like-minded mothers who understand the joys and struggles of raising a child. Connecting with other moms allows me to share experiences, seek advice, and gain a broader perspective on the journey of motherhood. It reminds me that I am not alone and that we are all navigating this beautiful but sometimes challenging path together.

In the process of finding joy in the real, I have come to appreciate the significance of balance. Motherhood is a delicate dance between caring for our children and caring for ourselves. It is about finding harmony between our roles as mothers and our identities as individuals. It's about recognizing that our well-being matters and that by taking care of ourselves, we are ultimately better able to care for those we love.

So, I commit to carving out moments of self-care amidst the chaos. I commit to embracing the support of my fellow mothers and cherishing the connections we forge. I commit to celebrating my own journey, with all its ups and downs, and finding joy in the real, imperfect, and beautiful moments that define my experience of motherhood.In my ongoing quest to find joy in the real, I have also learned to embrace the power of mindfulness and gratitude. It's easy to get caught up in the whirlwind of everyday tasks and responsibilities, often overlooking the small miracles and blessings that surround us.

Mindfulness is the practice of being fully present in the current moment, without judgment or attachment. It is about cultivating a deep awareness of our thoughts, emotions, and sensations as they arise. By bringing mindfulness into my experience of motherhood, I have found that even the most mundane tasks can become opportunities for joy and connection.

Whether it's changing a diaper, preparing a meal, or playing on the floor, I strive to approach these activities with a sense of presence and intention. I immerse myself in the sensory details—the softness of my baby's skin, the aroma of her shampoo, the sound of her laughter—and let them anchor me in the here and now. By doing so, I am able to fully engage with my baby and create moments of genuine connection and joy.

Gratitude is another powerful tool that has transformed my perspective on motherhood. It is a practice of acknowledging and appreciating the abundance in our lives, no matter how small or seemingly insignificant. Instead of dwelling on what I lack or the challenges I face, I focus on the blessings that surround me.

Every day, I take a few moments to reflect on the things I am grateful for as a mother. It might be the way my baby's tiny fingers curl around mine, the sound of her first attempts at saying "mama," or the warmth of her embrace. It could be the support of my partner or the love and guidance of my own mother. It might even be the simple pleasure of witnessing my baby explore and discover the world with wide-eyed wonder.

By cultivating mindfulness and gratitude, I have found that even in the most challenging moments of motherhood, there is always something to be grateful for. It could be a lesson learned, a strength discovered, or a bond deepened. It's about shifting my focus from what may be missing or difficult to what is present and beautiful.

As I continue on this journey of finding joy in the real, I embrace mindfulness and gratitude as invaluable companions. They serve as reminders to slow down, appreciate the simple moments, and be fully present with my baby. They encourage me to celebrate the small victories, cherish the fleeting stages of childhood, and find joy in the ordinary and extraordinary aspects of being a mother.

In the end, it is through mindfulness, gratitude, self-care, and genuine connection that I have truly discovered the depths of joy in motherhood. It is in the messy, imperfect, and authentic moments that I find the greatest happiness—the joy that comes from loving and being loved by my precious child.

~ The Triumphant mom ~

Conclusion:

In a world dominated by hashtags and filters, the Instagram moms realize that their babies should be more than just an accessory for a perfect feed. True motherhood lies in the messy moments, the laughter, the tears, and the imperfections that make each child unique. It's a journey of self-discovery and self-acceptance, where the worth of their babies is not defined by virtual likes but by the love, care, and genuine connection they share. The Instagram moms become an advocate for embracing authenticity, encouraging others to look beyond the filtered lens and find joy in the real, unscripted moments of motherhood.

In this age of digital validation, the Instagram moms' realization serves as a powerful reminder that motherhood is not about meeting societal expectations or striving for perfection. It's about nurturing and cherishing the precious bond between a mother and her child, irrespective of the standards set by social media. By embracing authenticity and celebrating the raw, unfiltered moments, the Instagram moms become an inspiration for others to break free from the confines of virtual validation and focus on what truly matters.

Through these moms' advocacy for genuine connection and self-acceptance, the Instagram moms encourage fellow mothers to resist the pressures of creating an idyllic online persona and instead embrace the beautiful chaos that comes with raising a child. They understand that the worth of her baby cannot be quantified by the number of likes or comments on a post, but rather by the love, care, and joy shared between them.

By stepping away from the curated world of social media, the Instagram moms rediscovers the profound joy in the simplest of moments – a messy playdate, a heartfelt giggle, or a quiet, tender embrace. She realizes that these are the moments that truly define motherhood and create lasting memories.

Ultimately, these Instagram moms evolve from being confined to the pressures of an idealized image and discover the beauty of embracing the authenticity of their own unique motherhood journey, both online and offline.

As they all continue their journey, the Instagram moms realize the importance of setting boundaries in the digital world. They become more mindful of screen time and establish designated moments for uninterrupted bonding with their child. The moms recognize that the memories created in those precious, unfiltered moments are far more valuable than the number of likes on a post.

With this new found perspective, the Instagram moms begin to share more candid glimpses into their lives, showcasing the messy realities and challenges of motherhood. They understand that by being vulnerable and authentic, they can inspire other moms who may be struggling with the same insecurities and pressures.

Instead of seeking validation from strangers on the internet, they focus on building a supportive community of like-minded individuals who understand the complexities of modern motherhood. These moms actively engage in meaningful conversations, offering and receiving support, empathy, and advice from other fellow moms.

As time goes on, the Instagram moms' profile becomes a space of empowerment and positivity. The instagram moms now use their socal platform to advocate for important issues surrounding motherhood, such as maternal mental health, work-life balance, and the importance of self-care. By sharing her own experiences and insights, she becomes a source of inspiration for others, reminding them that it's okay to embrace imperfections and prioritize their well-being.

Beyond the online realm, the Instagram moms become an active participant in their local community. They connect with other moms through playgroups, parenting workshops, and support networks. These moms realize that the real-life connections they foster are equally, if not more, fulfilling than virtual interactions.

Through their journeys, the Instagram moms find their voices and become an advocate for balance and self-acceptance. They encourage others to celebrate the diversity of motherhood, reminding them that every journey is unique and valid. By breaking free from the confines of societal expectations, they pave the way for a more inclusive and accepting portrayal of motherhood in the digital age.

In the end, the Instagram moms' journeys serve as a powerful reminder that social media can be a tool for empowerment and connection when used with intention and authenticity. By embracing the messiness of real-life moments and prioritizing genuine connections, they redefine what it means to be an Instagram mom, paving the way for a more balanced and fulfilling approach to modern motherhood.

In conclusion, the journey of the Instagram moms reflects a broader societal need to reevaluate our obsession with virtual validation and prioritize real, authentic connections. Through their transformation, these moms not only discover the true essence of motherhood but also become a guiding light for others to navigate the complexities of parenting in the digital age. By championing the value of imperfections and embracing the unfiltered reality, the Instagram moms leave an indelible mark, reminding us all to find joy in the unscripted and genuine moments of life.

Printed in Great Britain
by Amazon